MICHAEL DAHL PRESENTS

# The Minotaur Maze

by Thomas Kingsley Troupe

illustrated by Xavier Bonet

STONE ARCH BOOKS
a capstone imprint

Michael Dahl Presents is published by Stone Arch Books,
A Capstone Imprint
1710 Roe Crest Drive
North Mankato, Minnesota 56003
www.mycapstone.com

Library of Congress Cataloging-in-Publication Data is
available on the Library of Congress website.

Summary:
It's the assistant librarian's birthday! When the
Nightingale Library Pages surprise him, the shock is
theirs—a Minotaur has turned the library into a deadly
labyrinth! Theseus and Ariadne have entered the library
to help out. Can this Greek god and goddess help the
kids find their way out of this maze?

ISBN: 978-1-4965-7895-2 (hardcover)
ISBN: 978-1-4965-7899-0 (eBook PDF)

Printed and bound in the USA.
042019   001965

① **Ask an adult to download the app.**

 Capstone 4D
Education

② **Scan any page with the star.**

③ **Enjoy your cool stuff!**

—————— OR ——————

Use this password at capstone4D.com

maze.78952

# MICHAEL DAHL PRESENTS

Michael Dahl has written about werewolves, magicians, and superheroes. He loves funny books, scary books, and mysterious books. Every Michael Dahl Presents book is chosen by Michael himself and written by an author he loves. The books are about favorite subjects like monster aliens, haunted houses, farting pigs, or magical powers that go haywire. Read on!

# Midnight Library

LIBRARY

The **MIDNIGHT LIBRARY** was named after T. Middleton Nightingale, or "Mid Night." More than 100 years ago, Nightingale built the library but then vanished. The giant clock in the library went silent. Its hands froze at twelve. Since that day, no one has heard the clock chime again. Except for the librarian Javier and his team of young Pages. Whenever they hear it strike twelve, the library transforms. The world inside a book becomes real—along with its dangers. Whether it's mysteries to be solved or threats to be defeated, it's up to the librarian and his Pages to return the Midnight Library to normal.

### The Librarian

JAVIER O'LEARY — Javier is supervisor of the library's Page program.

## The Pages

BARU REDDY — He reads a lot of horror books. And his memory is awesome.

JORDAN YOUNG — Her parents have banned video games for the summer. She hopes working at the library might get her access to gaming on the library computers.

KELLY GENDELMAN — She figures helping at the library will be fun. Maybe the other Pages will appreciate her love of bad puns.

CAL PETERSON — His parents think the library is a good place to expose him to more books. They never expected him to go *inside* a book!

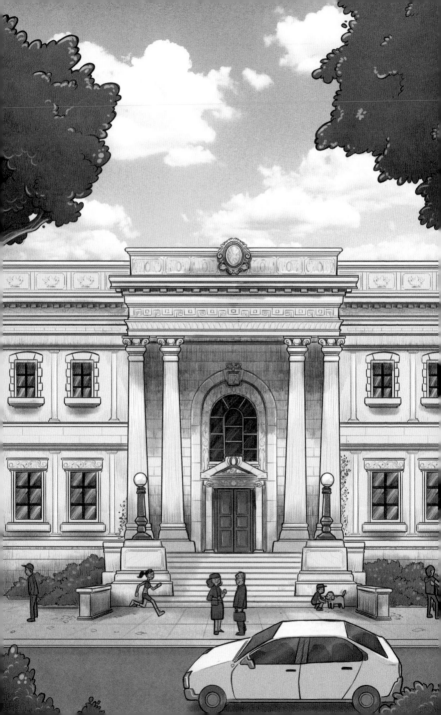

# CHAPTER ONE
# Running Late

Kelly Gendelman ran down the busy sidewalk. She was carrying a large box from 5th Street Sweets. The line had been ridiculous. Now she was over an hour late for her Saturday shift at the T. Middleton Nightingale City Library.

As she approached 13th Avenue, the light

changed. She'd have to wait for the next walk signal.

An older woman with a large purse smiled kindly at her. She eyed the fancy light blue box Kelly was holding. "What's the hurry, dear?" the woman asked.

"I'm late for my . . . job," Kelly said. She kept her eyes on the crosswalk signal. "It's my boss's birthday. I offered to pick up treats."

*Weird to say I have a job and a boss,* Kelly thought. *Especially since I'm in middle school.*

She was a volunteer Page at the library, which meant she didn't get paid. And Javier, the librarian who ran the program, hardly acted like a boss.

"Take your time," the woman said. "Those goodies will taste just as good no matter when you get there."

"Thanks," Kelly said. She exhaled, trying to relax. "And you're right."

Even so, as soon as she saw the *WALK* signal, Kelly took off across 13th.

To tell the truth, she wasn't worried about getting in trouble with Javier. She just wanted to get to the library before everything changed.

T. Middleton Nightingale Library, or the "Midnight Library" as they liked to call it, had a strange secret. Every Saturday at noon it went through a *change*. Somehow the library shifted into a world resembling a place from one of the library's hundreds of thousands of books. Javier said it was like being "inside the mind of an author." Javier and the Pages, however, were the only ones who experienced the change.

Kelly glanced at the time on the First Bank and Trust sign. *11:56!* she thought. *I was supposed to be there over an hour ago!*

She ran around a pair of strollers clogging up the sidewalk. She bumped into a guy carrying a briefcase who was talking on his phone. With another glance over her shoulder, she saw that another minute had ticked by.

"Three minutes!" she whispered. She caught a few strange looks from people nearby. She could see the big steps and ornate statues ahead.

Kelly ran. She could feel the treats inside the box shift around. She weaved through more foot traffic, apologizing as she went. At long last she reached the big stone staircase. Kelly dashed up the stairs and flung open the heavy front door. She had barely a minute to spare. Rolene, the information desk librarian, looked up from a small book.

"Oh my, Ms. Gendelman," Rolene said quickly. "We were all pretty sure you wouldn't be joining us today."

"The line at the bakery was ridiculous," Kelly replied. She struggled to catch her breath. "*Donut* they know I have somewhere to be?"

Rolene raised her eyebrows a bit.

Kelly glanced around the enormous library. "Where is everyone?"

"I believe they're out on the floor, shelf reading or shelving," Rolene said.

"Thanks," Kelly said. Then she dashed into the library's huge common area.

In the middle of the library stood the enormous, ancient clock. The hands were forever stuck at midnight . . . or noon. No one was quite sure.

*Of course they didn't wait for me,* Kelly thought. *I'm almost an hour and a half . . .*

Just then, she heard the gong of a distant clock.

"Late," she said aloud, finishing her thought.

*Here we go,* Kelly thought. She set the box of birthday treats down on an empty table.

Kelly frantically looked through the shelves, hoping to spot at least one of the other Pages.

*Where were Baru, Jordan, and Cal? Where was Javier?*

The clock gonged eleven more times.

. . . And everything around her changed.

CHAPTER TWO
# Princess Protector

The tables in the library turned into stone slabs. They dropped to the ground with a thundering boom. The bookshelves shifted and moved. They quickly reshaped into walls and corridors. The once-high ceiling dropped lower, making the space feel cramped.

Kelly shrieked when lit torches erupted

from the wall sconces. The flames lit the dim passageways with flickering orange light. Nothing around Kelly looked familiar. All she could see ahead of her was a passageway that led into darkness. There was a sour smell, like a wet, filthy animal. She plugged her nose briefly, hoping the stink would go away. It didn't.

More than ever, she wished her fellow Pages were there.

"Where am I?" Kelly whispered. She touched a stone wall.

"This is the Labyrinth," came a voice from behind her. "Did King Aegeus not tell you of your fate?"

A girl stepped out from the shadows. She looked about eighteen. The girl had long, reddish hair that fell to her shoulders. Unlike the T-shirt and jeans Kelly wore, the girl was in a fancy, white dress. She didn't look like any of the library visitors. It didn't take Kelly long to realize who it was.

"You're Ariadne," Kelly whispered. "Daughter of King Minos, ruler of Crete."

"And you're one of the fourteen sacrifices, are you not?" Ariadne replied. She seemed a little surprised as she looked Kelly up and down. "You don't dress like others from Athens."

"I'm from Queens," Kelly said.

"Ah. So you're a princess as well," Ariadne said. "Are you the daughter of Medea?"

"No, I'm the daughter of Deborah,"

Kelly said. "I did a history project on Ancient Greece, but I don't remember who Medea is."

Ariadne looked confused.

"OK," Kelly said. "Sorry. Long story short? I'm not from Athens. And I wasn't sent here by King Aegeus."

"Then you must help me, stranger," Ariadne said.

"It's Kelly," Kelly said. She pointed to herself. "That's my name."

"Yes, Kelly of Queens," Ariadne said quickly. Kelly's name seemed to be the least of her worries. "I fear we're running out of time. I need to find Theseus and lead him out of here."

"I remember that name," Kelly said. "That's

the guy you like! He was one of the fourteen that your father had run through the maze as a sacrifice to—"

From somewhere far into the Labyrinth, a deep, loud growl vibrated the stone walls.

"—the Minotaur," Kelly finished in a whisper. "Big, ugly, half-bull, half-human creature. Right?"

Ariadne nodded. "You know of the hunter! I am impressed."

"My project kind of rocked," Kelly said.

Ariadne crouched down. She seemed to be feeling the ground for something. The hem of her white dress dipped into a dirty puddle.

"What are you looking for?" Kelly asked, moving closer to Ariadne.

"Theseus," the princess replied. "I left a thread for him to follow so he could find his way out."

There was another growl nearby. Then came a loud snort.

"It sounds like the Minotaur's getting closer," Kelly said. Then she remembered something. "Does he still carry that axe?"

"Oh yes," Ariadne said. She suddenly gasped in excitement.

"What?" Kelly asked, nervously eyeing the dim hallway. "What is it?"

"The thread," Ariadne said. "I've found it!

The princess stood up. She shouted down one of the hallways. "Hold tight, my beloved! I'll find you!" Then she took off.

Kelly stood frozen in place. She couldn't decide what was a better idea. Should she follow Ariadne deeper into the Labyrinth? Or should she try to find her friends on her own?

The princess was following the thread down a passageway. A moment later she heard the heavy clomps of hooves on stone.

*The Minotaur!*

"Wait up! I'm coming with you!" Kelly shouted.

CHAPTER THREE
# Stone Cold

Kelly and Ariadne dashed down the dim hallway. The princess followed the thread through the corridors. Each time Kelly passed a torch, she ducked. She didn't want to set her hair on fire. They turned left down two passageways and went down a small set of steps. Then they passed three other openings and turned right into another dark chamber.

"I am so lost," Kelly whispered as they came to a stop. She couldn't tell which way they'd come. If she had to get back to where they'd started, she'd never get there.

"As we all are," Ariadne replied. She held up the thread.

Kelly squinted. The thread was severed. "So what happened?" she asked.

"Something must've happened to Theseus," Ariadne whispered. "I gave him a sword to fight off the foul beast. I had hoped he could defeat the Minotaur. Then he could follow this thread and find his way out."

Kelly felt panic rise in her chest. They were trapped in a dark maze with the

Minotaur—and who knew what else. She took a step. Something clattered in the dark along the floor. She bent down to see what it was. Her hand touched something metallic. She ran her hand along the object and found a handle. With a grunt, she lifted it up.

"Was this the sword?" Kelly asked. The torchlight made the steel glint.

"By the gods," Ariadne said. "Yes. That's the very weapon I entrusted to Theseus!"

A heavy silence fell between them. *This is not good*, thought Kelly.

Ariadne took the sword from Kelly. She inspected the blade in the dim light.

Kelly listened carefully. She could hear hooves clomping heavily along the stone passageways.

"This sword saw no battle," Ariadne whispered. "The edges are as sharp as ever."

"So maybe he dropped it," Kelly said. "Whatever happened, we need to get out of here."

Kelly moved to the wall and picked up the flaming torch. Then she walked toward the middle of the room, lighting the way.

As she did, she saw several faces staring back at her.

"Whoa!" Kelly gasped, almost dropping the torch. "Um . . . come here for a second!"

The princess turned her attention away from the sword and joined Kelly.

Kelly held the torch out in front of them. There were several gray stone statues of men.

Their eyes and mouths were open wide as if caught in mid-scream. All of them looked incredibly lifelike.

And Kelly recognized one of them. "Javier," she gasped. Her heart sank. "Oh no." She reached out and touched the statue's arm. Javier looked out of place. The other statues were dressed like ancient Greek warriors. One of them wore a helmet with what looked like the bristles of a hairbrush across the top. Another wore a small crown of leaves on his head. He held a shield across his chest. Javier, however, was wearing his usual dress pants and button-down shirt.

Ariadne put her fingers on the cheek of the helmeted statue.

"Is that . . . ?" Kelly began.

"Theseus," Ariadne whispered.

Kelly put her hand on the princess's shoulder.

"No sculptor could carve statues so lifelike as these," Ariadne said. "They have been turned to stone." A single tear streaked down her face.

*So that's it,* Kelly thought. *That's the end of Javier and these Greek guys.*

Suddenly, before either of them had time to grieve, a snorting beast burst through the doorway.

## CHAPTER FOUR
# Just a Minotaur

Ariadne's sadness was quickly replaced with rage. "Minotaur!" she shouted.

The beast was enormous. He had the head of a snarling, angry bull. He looked like a giant of a man. The Minotaur had bulging muscles and large, powerful hands. His long, twisted horns nearly scraped the stone ceiling. He growled and snorted as he tightened his grip on the gigantic axe.

With a roar, Minotaur raised the mighty weapon above his head. Kelly had a horrifying thought. *He's going to smash the statues!*

Without thinking, Kelly swung the torch, catching the Minotaur in the armpit.

The monster bellowed in pain. A moment later, the smell of cooked meat hit Kelly's nose. The Minotaur lowered the axe. He swatted at the burn with his free hand.

Ariadne stepped forward, sword in hand.

"I've never fought a beast like this!" she shouted.

"Then let's get out of here!" Kelly cried.

The Minotaur howled. Kelly and Ariadne

ran across the room and into another dark passageway. They reached an intersection with three corridors to choose from.

"Which way?" Kelly shouted.

Without a word, Ariadne grabbed Kelly by the arm. She led her down the passage on the left. A thunderous roar echoed through the halls.

"I think he's upset with us," Kelly said. They barreled down another hallway. Bones from shattered skeletons lay on either side of them. A skull with empty eye sockets seemed to watch them as they ran by.

Kelly noticed that it was really dark. There weren't any torches other than the one she held. The Minotaur only had to follow their light to find them.

Ariadne slowed down at another

intersection. "Another choice to make," she said. "Left or right."

Kelly walked over to the right. A few feet ahead was a small doorway. Crumbled columns on either side held up the low ceiling. She stepped through to find a small square-shaped room. More bones and tattered rags were scattered along the floor. Kelly guessed they were the clothes of the Minotaur's victims.

"Dead end," Kelly whispered. "In more ways than one."

"The other passage continues deeper into the Labyrinth," Ariadne said. "A foul wind blows from there."

*I don't think we have much choice,* Kelly thought. *We have yet to see an exit!*

Loud, angry snorts approached. It was just

as Kelly had feared. The Minotaur had seen their light. He knew exactly where they were.

"We have to get rid of our torch so the Minotaur can't track us," Kelly whispered. "But I have a plan."

Kelly took a deep breath and threw the torch into the mess of bones and cloth. She and Ariadne backed into a passageway, but Kelly held Ariadne's arm to keep her from running away. They watched as the pile caught fire.

Ariadne turned to her. "We must flee, Kelly from Queens," she said urgently.

"Not yet," Kelly said. "First we need to stop this bull-headed beast."

Kelly didn't dare breathe. The monster approached. He turned to follow the light into the small room filled with bones and fire.

"OK," Kelly said. "Now!"

She raced toward the columns outside
of the room. Ariadne followed close
behind."Smash these things!" Kelly cried.
"With everything you've got!"

They kicked at the crumbling columns,
loosening chunks of rock. The ceiling above
them rumbled a bit.

The Minotaur turned around and roared
again.

"He sees us, Queens Kelly!" Ariadne
shouted.

"Good," Kelly shouted back. "Let's see if
he's as pea-brained as he looks!"

The Minotaur wound his axe back behind
his head. With both hands, he swung at the

girls. Kelly jumped back at the last second. The heavy blade hit the old column. The stones crumbled and fell—and with them fell the stone ceiling they supported.

Kelly and Ariadne staggered back. The entire doorway was buried in rubble. The Minotaur was trapped inside the room.

"That should column him down," Kelly joked.

Ariadne didn't laugh.

"Whatever," Kelly said. "Let's keep moving."

# CHAPTER FIVE

# Pay the Python

Kelly and Ariadne moved through a series of dark corridors. Finally they found a long hallway lit brightly along both sides with torches.

"So your dad did all this?" Kelly asked. "He made young people from Athens go through this Labyrinth so the Minotaur could get them?"

Ariadne sighed. "Yes. He did it to avenge the death of Androgeus, my brother. Androgeus competed in the Athens games and was killed. Every seven years since, Father has ordered seven boys and seven girls to navigate the Labyrinth as a sacrifice."

"That seems a bit extreme," Kelly said.

Ariadne nodded. "That's why I wanted to help Theseus put an end to this."

*But now he, Javier, and those other warriors have been turned to stone,* Kelly thought.

They were suddenly interrupted by voices further down the hallway.

"Who's down there?"

Kelly instantly recognized the voice.

"Cal?" she cried.

A moment later, Cal and the two other Nightingale Pages, Baru and Jordan, stepped out from the shadows. "Kelly!" Baru cried. He ran down the hall toward her and Ariadne. "I'm so happy to see you!"

"Yeah," Jordan said, following him. "Where were you?"

With all of the Pages reunited, Kelly explained her delay at the bakery. She told them how she'd been alone when the library changed. Then Kelly introduced everyone to Ariadne.

"And I found Javier," Kelly said sadly. "He was turned into a statue. Along with Theseus and some other ancient warriors."

"Oh no," Cal said. "One of the other guys was Perseus. There were all going to fight the monsters in here and come get us when it was safe."

*Perseus,* Kelly thought. *That name sounds familiar. But did Cal just say . . . monsters? As in more than one?*

"We've defeated the Minotaur," Ariadne said. "Thanks to the quick thinking of Queens Kelly here."

"You said monsters, Cal," Kelly said. "What else is in here?"

Jordan nodded. "This place is crawling with bad stuff," she said. "Like—"

There was a loud hiss. The floor rumbled beneath their feet. Something heavy was coming. Kelly watched the darkness carefully. They all gasped when a monstrous face appeared in the orange torchlight.

"It looks like a dragon," Baru whispered.

"That is Python," Ariadne said. "He is an earth dragon from the center of our world. Apollo himself seeks to hunt the beast. He wants revenge for his mother, the goddess Leto."

*Wow,* Kelly thought. *Ancient Greece is full of revenge, nastiness, and monsters.*

Python drew closer, its eyes narrowed, as it caught sight of Kelly and her crew. It opened its mouth to display rows of sharp and deadly teeth.

"Behind me, friends of Kelly!" Ariadne shouted. She raised the sword she'd given to Theseus.

Kelly watched as the creature moved closer. It cocked its head back and belched forth a

stream of flame. Ariadne cut through the fire with her sword. She sent flames off to either side to warm the stone walls.

Even so, Kelly felt the heat on her skin. She didn't think this was a battle Ariadne could win. Apollo, the god of sun and light, hadn't defeated Python. What chance did the mortal daughter of King Minos have?

The sword was glowing red, as if it had trapped the heat of the monster's fiery breath.

Ariadne swung it at the creature, but Python swatted the blow away like it was nothing. With a roar, the dragon rose up onto its back legs and pounded the ground. In an instant, the floor gave way. Kelly and the rest of the crew fell into a dank, dark cavern below.

CHAPTER SIX
# Trapped!

"Now we're in trouble," Cal said as he rose to his feet.

"And wet," Baru said, standing up. Water dripped from his soaked shirt and pants.

They'd landed in a heap in a small, wet cave beneath the Labyrinth.

Kelly needed a moment to catch her breath. She looked up at the hole in the cavern ceiling. Torches continued to burn above them. A moment later, Python peered down.

"We have to get up," Jordan said. She stood above Kelly and offered her a hand. "We're not out of the maze yet."

Kelly took Jordan's hand and got to her feet. On the other side of the cave, Ariadne was splashing through the small pool of water. She was looking for a way out.

"We are trapped," she said. She looked up at the leering earth dragon. "That monster has us right where he wants us."

Kelly kept her eyes on the dragon. All it had to do was come down and start eating them. But for some reason . . . it didn't.

"What's Python waiting for?" Kelly asked. As if in reply, the dragon unleashed another blast of fire. Again Ariadne stepped in front of the blast and split the flame with the sword. The sword was now glowing orange. Ripples of heat blurred the air around the blade.

"It's trying to cook us first," Cal said. "Great. Just great!"

Python leaned into the hole, and everyone backed up against the wall. They crowded behind a cluster of stalagmites to hide. The beast's nose was barely a foot off the ground. It seemed to be sniffing for them.

*Maybe it's getting tired of trying to set us on fire and just wants to eat already,* Kelly thought.

Feeling the heat from the glowing sword,

Kelly was struck with another idea. She leaned toward Ariadne and whispered to her.

The princess looked at Kelly. For the first time since they'd met, she smiled.

"Let us try this plan, Kelly of Queens." She turned to the others. "Stay here," she whispered.

The two of them dashed out toward the pool of water and the dragon's head.

"What are you two doing?" Baru shouted.

*Watch and see,* Kelly thought.

She and Ariadne split up. The princess stood near a large puddle of water. Kelly stopped just a few feet from the dragon's snout. She watched as the beast's eyes locked with hers. It seemed somewhat confused

and unsure of what was happening. But Kelly knew it could snap and eat her at any moment.

"You've got a real case of dragon breath," she said.

Python reared its head back, ready to unleash another flame. As it did, a loud hissing sound filled the cavern. Ariadne was lowering her sword into the pool of water. Almost instantly the small cave filled with steam. It was impossible for Python to see.

"Now, Queens Kelly!" Ariadne yelled.

Kelly dove out of the way, sticking a perfect somersault. Ariadne advanced and drove the sword through the earth dragon's throat. With a massive groan, Python's head slumped to the ground.

When the steam cleared, Kelly and Ariadne stood in front of the foul beast, looking like warriors.

"Are you serious?" Cal shouted. "You guys are incredible!"

Kelly caught her breath and smiled at her friends. Ariadne wiped the blood off of her blade on her battle-damaged dress.

"And now we have a way out of here," Baru said, pointing.

It was true. The body of the monster was still up in the Labyrinth, but its neck and head extended down to the cavern floor.

"Thanks, Python!" Jordan shouted.

The five of them climbed up the dragon's neck to get out of the cave. As Kelly emerged, she half-expected the library to turn back to its original state. When it didn't, she realized there was still more for them to do before they could go back home.

At least she hoped they still *could* get back home.

# CHAPTER SEVEN

# Not a Good Look

Once they were back in the Labyrinth, Kelly looked at everyone. They were all wet, a bit scuffed up, and looked exhausted.

"Maybe we just need to get out of the Labyrinth now," Cal said. "Do you know the way, Ariadne?"

The princess shook her head. "The only

soul who knows the way out is the Minotaur," she said quietly.

"Yeah," Kelly said. "And we're not asking him."

The group headed out of the broken corridor, leaving Python's lifeless body behind. They walked through a series of twisting passages. At long last, they ended up in a room with large flaming braziers. Fire burned from the metal containers, lighting the room. Large, decorative pools of water lined a walkway that led to a magnificent set of stone steps. Beautiful white columns rose to the ceiling. All around the room were statues of warriors, their arms and shields raised in battle.

"Is this the exit?" Cal asked.

He ran toward the stairs in excitement, and Jordan followed. Kelly felt hopeful as she looked around the majestic room. It *did* look different from the rest of the Labyrinth.

Just as she was about to run after her friends, she heard it. A loud rattling sound, followed by the sound of something heavy slithering across the floor.

Something sinister emerged out of the shadows. Kelly, Baru, and Ariadne ran over to hide behind a couple of warrior statues. Kelly almost shouted to warn Cal and Jordan, but she couldn't find her voice.

A monster with the torso of a woman and the tail of a snake weaved through the columns. She held a bow in one hand and had a quiver of arrows slung over her back.

The end of her tail looked like that of a rattlesnake. Through the shadows, Kelly could see large things squirming around the woman's head.

Ariadne whispered, "I think it's—"

"Medusa," Kelly interrupted as it all came back to her. "If you look into her eyes, she'll turn you to stone."

"She's fascinating," Baru said, moving toward her.

Baru loved monsters, but Medusa was not a creature to be admired. Ariadne waved her hands and gestured for him to get back behind the soldier.

*I have to warn Cal and Jordan before it's too late!* Kelly thought, her mind racing.

Kelly watched helplessly as Cal and Jordan reached the steps.

*We have to do something,* Kelly thought. *But what? If any of us catch her gaze, we're doomed!*

If she called out, they would turn around and make eye contact with the monster. The only chance to protect Cal and Jordan was to somehow distract Medusa.

As Cal and Jordan began to climb the steps, they turned as if to urge the others to join them. As they did, both of the Pages caught site of Medusa. Cal's mouth opened in horror, and Jordan tried to shield her eyes. It didn't matter.

Instantly both of the Nightingale Library Pages were turned to solid stone.

While Medusa was still facing Jordan and Cal, Baru hurried over to join Kelly and Ariadne. As Kelly was about to cry out, Ariadne pulled her back further into the shadows.

Kelly felt tears starting to form in the corners of her eyes.

*Pull yourself together, Kelly,* she thought. *Crying isn't going to get you anywhere!*

"She made them statues like Javier and those other guys," Baru whispered. "This is terrible. We are in serious trouble."

Kelly heard the rattle of Medusa's tail as the creature slithered around the room.

"What can we do, Kelly from Queens?" Ariadne asked. "Have you another idea this time?"

"I'm thinking," Kelly whispered. She tried to remember what she knew about Medusa, and realized it was Perseus who had defeated the snake-headed fiend in Greek mythology. He'd used a mirrored shield and some flying boots to sneak up on the wicked monster and cut off her head.

"She's going to find us," Baru said. "I don't want to become a statue like the others!"

*That gives me an idea,* Kelly thought. She brought the others close and whispered her plan to them. Ariadne and Baru nodded in silent agreement.

It was a long shot, but Kelly thought it might be their only chance.

# CHAPTER EIGHT

# Apollo, Gee

Medusa's serpent body slid across the stone floor, closer and closer to them.

Using the sword, Kelly quickly cut two long strips of cloth from the end of Ariadne's damp and dirty dress. She first tied one strip around Baru's eyes, making a blindfold.

"No matter what, don't take this off!"
Kelly said.

As planned, Baru crawled away, feeling
his way to another part of Medusa's room.
Kelly took the remaining strip of cloth and
blindfolded herself. She heard Ariadne
whisper in her ear.

"Good luck, my friend."

Then Kelly heard the warrior princess
sneak away in the opposite direction. Unable
to see and scared out of her mind, Kelly
stayed put.

"Hey, snake head!" Baru shouted from the
other side of the room. "Aim those creepy
eyes of yours this way!"

Medusa made a horrible hissing sound, and
her rattle twitched in anger. The sound of her

slithering was louder and more frantic, as if she were rushing over toward Baru.

It was time for Kelly to do her part. She stood up, just as she'd told Baru to do when he was in position. Her heart rattled around in her ribs like the end of Medusa's tail.

"Over here, you fork-tongued fiend!" Kelly shouted. "You're not so tough when your eyes can't do anything, are you?"

She heard Medusa fit an arrow into her bow. There was a creak of the wooden bow as the monster drew the arrow back.

*Forgot about the bow and arrow,* Kelly thought. *I just hope I bought Ariadne enough time!*

There was a *twang,* and Kelly froze in place, almost certain an arrow would hit her at any second. There was a rush of air past her left ear, then a clatter against the wall behind her. A second clatter told her the arrow had fallen to the ground.

Then came another creak. Kelly knew Medusa was about to take another shot. Without warning, there was a battle cry followed by a heavy *thump* on the ground.

Kelly stood blindfolded, unsure what had happened. Was Ariadne still alive? Had Medusa turned her to stone too?

"Remove your eye coverings, Queens Kelly and Baru boy," Ariadne said. "It is over."

Kelly pulled off her blindfold. Ariadne was standing over the headless body of Medusa. She motioned for Kelly to bring her strip of fabric over.

"Don't look," the princess warned. "Her eyes can still turn you to stone."

As Ariadne tied one of the blindfolds across Medusa's eyes, a bright light exploded from the doorway. A large man emerged. He had hair that shone like the sun. Kelly instantly knew who he was.

"Apollo," Kelly whispered.

"Greetings, mortals!" the Greek god boomed. "I've come to slay Python once and for all!"

"Already took care of that," Baru said.

"And Medusa, I see," Apollo said approvingly. "You have been busy."

"Theseus was to defeat the Minotaur, but Kelly of Queens trapped him in his own maze," Ariadne said. "Theseus, along with others, were turned to stone. While we are proud of our deeds, they have come at a mighty cost."

The glowing god nodded. "Let me see what I can do," Apollo said.

The entire Labyrinth exploded with a burst of pure, glowing sunlight. Kelly closed her eyes and felt herself revived. She smiled as she remembered that Apollo was not only the god of light and the sun. He also had the ability to heal.

*But can Apollo heal people who have been turned to stone?* Kelly wondered.

As the light warmed her face, she heard the distant single gong of the clock. The library was changing back!

Kelly opened her eyes, but it was still too bright to see.

*No!* Kelly thought as the world around her disappeared. *We can't go back without the others!*

As the sounds and smells of the Labyrinth faded away, Kelly heard Ariadne's voice one last time.

"Safe travels, Queens Kelly. Thank you for fighting with me. . . ."

# Epilogue

A moment later, Kelly opened her eyes. She was standing next to Baru in the T. Middleton Nightingale City Library. All of the library visitors went about their business of reading and looking for books as if nothing had happened.

Kelly looked at a clock on the wall. It was 12:01 p.m. Just like every time before, only a minute had passed.

"Oh no," Kelly said, looking at Baru. "Only the two of us made it. We have to go back!"

Baru looked confused. "I don't know how that is possible, Kelly."

"Then the others are trapped there as statues," Kelly said. "Apollo's magic didn't work. We've lost Cal, Jordan, and Javier forever!"

"Give the god some credit," a familiar girl's voice called from behind.

When Kelly turned, she saw Cal and Jordan standing up from behind a table.

"That was weird," Cal said. "Pretty sure I never want to get turned to stone again."

Kelly and Baru rushed over to greet their friends and give them hugs. Though they'd run into trouble during their journeys to other worlds within the Midnight Library, none of the journeys had been as perilous as their adventure with Ariadne.

"Oh no," Cal said sadly. "Look."

The four of them looked down at the nearby table. The light blue box from 5th Street Sweets was still there. They hadn't had the chance to celebrate Javier's birthday.

Jordan sighed. "Maybe Apollo's magic didn't reach far enough into the Labyrinth or—"

"Are those for me?" a voice called from above.

"It's Javier," Baru said. "Speaking to us from the afterlife!"

"No!" Javier shouted. "I'm up here!"

The Pages looked up. Leaning over the railing was their smiling mentor.

"Yes!" Kelly shouted in victory. "Happy birthday, Javier! Come down here so we can eat!"

In minutes the group was opening the box of delicious treats. They went over their adventures, detailing their many battles and close calls.

Once they'd had their fill of donuts and stories, the Pages went back to work. Kelly was assigned the 200 shelves in the Dewey Decimal system.

As she headed toward her assignment to begin shelving for the rest of the afternoon, she spotted a thread along the ground. It was almost invisible, but seemed to shine when the light hit it just right. Kelly picked it up and noticed that it ran the length of the aisle.

*Ariadne!*

She followed the thread and stopped in section 292, Roman and Greek Mythology. The thread went up the shelf. It was tied to a small envelope, sealed with wax. The symbol on the wax looked like a maze.

Kelly smiled. Then she tore open the envelope and read the letter inside. It was written in a fancy script with dark ink.

*Kelly of Queens,*

*Many thanks to you and your brave band of heroes! Thanks to our deeds, Apollo granted life once again to your friends, to Perseus, and to my beloved Theseus. None of them could believe*

*we defeated the Minotaur. They were impressed that we felled both Python and Medusa as well.*

*My father has closed the Labyrinth for good. No more sacrifices shall be made! Perseus asked if he could keep Medusa's head. He said it was going be a wedding gift. Odd fellow, that one.*

*May the gods shine upon you for the rest of your days!*

*Your friend,*

*Ariadne*

Kelly folded the letter and tucked it into her pocket. She was glad she'd made it to the library in time.

*An adventure like that?* Kelly thought. *I couldn't afford to myth it.*

# INSIDE THE MIDNIGHT MIND OF . . .
## the Gods and Heroes of Ancient Greece

When the Midnight clock chimes, the library transforms.
Javier says each of these transformations takes the library
"inside the mind of a book or writer." In this a-MAZE-ing
adventure, the Pages beam into a genre: Greek mythology. They
visit a world where the gods are real, but so are the monsters.

## Labyrinth & Minotaur

King Minos of Crete once stole a bull from the sea-god Poseidon. Poseidon cursed the king, and created a monstrous half-man and half-bull—the Minotaur. Minos ordered the clever inventor Daedalus to build the Labyrinth as an underground prison for the man-eating beast. Daedalus almost made the maze too good. When he had finished it and then inspected it, he had trouble getting out!

## Ariadne

Princess Ariadne, daughter of King Minos, is the only person who ever figured out a way to escape the Labyrinth. She gave Theseus a ball of thread that unraveled behind him as he walked through the maze. He could retrace his steps with the thread, like Hansel and Gretel did with their famous breadcrumbs. Years later, Ariadne married a Greek god and went to live on Mount Olympus.

## Medusa the Gorgon

The Gorgons were a fearful-looking trio born to Echidna, the "mother of all monsters." Medusa was the youngest. Unlike her sisters, she was the only mortal. Snakes grew on her head in place of hair. Anyone who looked into her flashing eyes turned to stone. After Perseus killed her, new creatures sprang out of her blood. One of the creatures was the powerful flying horse, Pegasus.

## Apollo

Apollo is the Greek and Roman god of the sun. He seems to have been extremely busy since he was also the god of healing, music, truth, poetry, prophecy, and all light. Oh, and he could cause plagues with his bow and arrows. Every day he drove his golden chariot across the sky pulled by four flaming horses. His twin sister is Artemis, goddess of the moon.

*Michael Dahl*

# Glossary

**afterlife** (AF-tur-life)—an existence after death

**avenge** (uh-VENJ)—to harm or punish someone who has harmed you or someone or something you care about

**brazier** (bra-ZEER)—a pan for holding burning coals

**entrusted** (en-TRUHST-id)—gave something valuable to someone to take care of

**intersection** (in-tur-SEK-shuhn)—the point at which two things meet and cross each other

**mortal** (MOR-tuhl)—not able to live forever

**ornate** (or-NAYT)—covered with a lot of decorations

**passageway** (PAS-ij-way)—an alley, a hallway, a tunnel, or anything that allows you to pass from one place to another

**perilous** (PER-uh-luhss)—dangerous

**sacrifice** (SAK-ruh-fyse)—the offering of something to a god

**stalagmite** (stuh-LAG-mite)—a tapering column that sticks up from the floor of a cave

# Discussion Questions

1.  How differently do you think things would have gone if Kelly wasn't late arriving at the library? Discuss some ways the story would have been different.
2.  Kelly sees her friends turned into stone statues. How would you feel if you were in her shoes seeing them in the labyrinth?
3.  Kelly's knowledge of Greek mythology helps the gang defeat Medusa. How would she be in trouble if she didn't know the stories of how Greek heroes stopped Medusa?

# Writing Prompts

1.  Ariadne sends Kelly a letter after their adventure. Write a response letter from Kelly's perspective thanking Ariadne for her help.
2.  Baru's love of monsters nearly gets him in trouble when he moves too close to Medusa. Write a version of the story where Baru is turned to stone along with Cal and Jordan. How differently would the story go?
3.  Imagine you went to the T. Middleton Nightingale City Library and were sent into the minotaur's labyrinth. Write a short scene about fighting a monster.

## about the author

Thomas Kingsley Troupe has been making up stories ever since he was in short pants. As an "adult" he's the author of a whole lot of books for kids. When he's not writing, he enjoys movies, biking, taking naps, and hunting ghosts as a member of the Twin Cities Paranormal Society. Raised in "Nordeast" Minneapolis, he now lives in Woodbury, Minnesota, with his awe-inspiring family.

## about the illustrator

Xavier Bonet is an illustrator and comic book artist who lives in Barcelona, Spain, with his wife and two children. He loves all retro stuff, video games, scary stories, and Mediterranean food, and cannot spend one hour without a pencil in his hand.